Stole

For show-and-tell Mari held up a beautiful white unicorn. "She's called Silvermane," Mari told the class. "The silver tail and mane are made from real horsehair."

"I can't believe it," Julia said. "I've wanted Silvermane ever since I saw her in the mall." She reached out to touch the shiny horn on the unicorn's head.

"No!" Mari snatched the unicorn away. "I'm not going to pass her around. Silvermane is too special."

Soon show-and-tell was over, and so was the rest of the afternoon. It was time to go home. But as the class was ready to leave, Mari cried out, "Silvermane! She's gone!"

The Nancy Drew Notebooks

1 The Slumber Party Secret
2 The Lost Locket
3 The Secret Santa
4 Bad Day for Ballet
5 The Soccer Shoe Clue
6 The Ice Cream Scoop
7 Trouble at Camp Treehouse
8 The Best Detective
9 The Thanksgiving Surprise
#10 Not Nice on Ice
#11 The Pen Pal Puzzle
#12 The Puppy Problem
#13 The Wedding Gift Goof
#14 The Funny Face Fight
#15 The Crazy Key Clue
#16 The Ski Slope Mystery
#17 Whose Pet Is Best?
#18 The Stolen Unicorn

Available from MINSTREL Books

For orders other than by individual consumers, Pocket Books grants a discount on the purchase of **10 or more** copies of single titles for special markets or premium use. For further details, please write to the Vice-President of Special Markets, Pocket Books, 1633 Broadway, New York, NY 10019-6785, 8th Floor.

For information on how individual consumers can place orders, please write to Mail Order Department, Simon & Schuster Inc., 200 Old Tappan Road, Old Tappan, NJ 07675.

#18

THE NANCY DREW NOTEBOOKS®

THE STOLEN UNICORN

CAROLYN KEENE

Illustrated by Anthony Accardo

PUBLISHED BY POCKET BOOKS

New York London Toronto Sydney Tokyo Singapore

This book is a work of fiction. Names, characters, places and incidents are products of the author's imagination or are used fictitiously. Any resemblance to actual events or locales or persons, living or dead, is entirely coincidental.

A MINSTREL PAPERBACK *Original*

A Minstrel Book published by
POCKET BOOKS, a division of Simon & Schuster Inc.
1230 Avenue of the Americas, New York, NY 10020

Produced by Mega-Books, Inc.

ISBN: 0-671-56862-0

First Minstrel Books printing May 1997

10 9 8 7 6 5 4 3 2 1

Cover art by Aleta Jenks

Printed in the U.S.A.

THE STOLEN UNICORN

1

The New Girl

"I have a secret," Alison Wegman told Nancy Drew during recess. Alison put her arm around her best friend, Brenda Carlton.

"And *you're* not allowed to know," Brenda said to Nancy. She twisted her dark hair around her finger and gave Nancy a mean smile.

"That's not fair," George Fayne said. She was Nancy's best friend. "I told you about my in-line skates before I showed them to the class."

"Okay. I'll give you a hint," Alison said. "It's silver and white, and it'll be the best show-and-tell you've ever seen."

Nancy rolled her eyes and looked at George. Alison was such a show-off.

It was show-and-tell week for the girls' third-grade class. Everyone had to bring in something from home to talk about in front of the group. Nancy wished they could have show-and-tell every week. It happened only four times a year.

"Hey, there's Bess with the new girl." George pointed across the schoolyard. "What's her name?"

Nancy waved to the two girls. "Mari Cheng."

Bess Marvin waved back as she and Mari headed toward the group. She was George's cousin and Nancy's other best friend. Bess was also Mari's "school buddy" for the week. That meant she was helping Mari get used to the way things were done at Carl Sandburg Elementary School.

"Mari seems pretty nice," Alison said. "My mom and I met her at the toy store last Saturday. I found out that

Mari was going to be in our class before anybody else did. I wonder what *she* has for show-and-tell."

"Who cares?" Brenda sneered. "She thinks she's too good for the rest of the class and won't talk to anybody."

Nancy crossed her arms. "Just because Mari's quiet doesn't mean she's stuck-up. Maybe she's shy."

"Give Mari a chance," George added. "After all, she's only been in Ms. Spencer's class since Monday."

Nancy's blue eyes twinkled. "You mean Mrs. Reynolds, not Ms. Spencer."

"Whoops." George put her hand over her mouth and laughed. "I keep forgetting our teacher is married now."

"Hi, guys!" Bess said when she and Mari reached the girls. "What's up?"

"Oh, nothing." Brenda looked at Mari and giggled. "We were just talking."

Nancy glared at Brenda. Then she turned to the new girl. "Hi, Mari."

"Hi," Mari said softly. She looked down at her shoes. Her shiny, black hair covered her face.

"So, Mari, what did you bring in for show-and-tell?" Alison asked. "Your row is up next."

Mari shrugged. "I—I brought . . . um . . . it's kind of . . ."

"She doesn't want to tell us," Brenda snapped.

"It isn't really a big thing." Mari's voice was so low, Nancy had to lean in closer to hear her. "It's—"

"You don't have to tell us if you don't want to," Alison broke in. "I'm keeping my show-and-tell a secret, too."

"Let me guess, Alison," Bess said. "Are you showing your new Flower Fairy perfume?"

"No," Alison said. "Even though I *am* the only one in class who has it. My surprise is even better." She turned to Mari. "Have you heard of Flower Fairy?"

Mari shook her head.

"I'm wearing it right now." Alison stuck out her arm. "Here, smell my wrist."

Mari was just leaning over to sniff Alison's wrist when Mike Minelli and Jason Hutchings came crashing into the group. The boys were in the middle of a game of tag and knocked Mari right to the ground.

"Hey, watch where you're going!" George shouted to the boys.

Nancy helped Mari back to her feet.

"Sorry," Jason said. He was laughing so hard, Nancy didn't think he sounded sorry.

"I forgot to tell you about Mike and Jason," Bess told Mari. "They're always starting trouble and playing dumb tricks."

"Our tricks aren't dumb," Mike said. "The people we play tricks on are dumb."

"That's right," Jason said. "We're

smart! We always have something up our sleeves. Don't we Mike?"

"Yup!" Mike grinned. "So you'd better watch out, Mari!"

Mari's eyes grew wide. "What do you mean?"

"You'll find out," Mike said. Then he tagged Jason. "You're it!" he yelled, running away.

Jason chased after him.

Later that afternoon Bess showed the class her fancy gold locket for show-and-tell. It was a gift from her aunt.

The day before, Nancy had shown a beautiful picture of her mother, who had died when Nancy was three years old. It was Nancy's favorite photograph.

Now it was Mari's turn. She walked slowly up the aisle holding a pink duffel bag. Her face was as red as a tomato.

Show-and-tell must be really hard for someone as shy as Mari, Nancy thought. I'll clap extra loud when she's done.

Mari put her bag on top of Julia Santos's desk, in the front of the room. Julia peeked inside Mari's bag.

"Awesome," Julia said.

One by one, Mari began taking seven beautiful toy horses out from her bag. "I love horses," she said. "My room is full of them. I have horse books, horse posters, horse videos—everything."

Nancy noticed that Mari seemed to like talking about something she loved.

"These horses are all different breeds and in all kinds of poses," Mari said, putting the last one on Julia's desk. Then she took something else out of her bag.

"This is my newest one. It isn't exactly a horse, but it's my favorite." Mari held up a beautiful white unicorn. "She's called Silvermane. The silver tail and mane are made from real horsehair that I can brush with

a special comb. She has her own stand, too."

Nancy had to smile when she saw Alison's mouth drop open at the sight of the unicorn. Even Brenda looked impressed.

"I can't believe it," Julia said out loud. "I've wanted Silvermane ever since I saw her in the mall." She reached out to touch the shiny horn on the unicorn's head.

"No!" Mari snatched it away. "I'm only going to pass around the other horses. Silvermane is too special."

"Sorry." Julia sank in her chair.

As Mari passed around the horses, Jason raised his hand.

"What do the horses do?" he asked Mari. "Do they walk? Do they fly?"

"Well, no," Mari said. "You have to use your imagination."

Jason pretended to yawn. "Borrrring!"

Mike jumped out of his seat. "But they *do* fly! See?" He tossed two toy horses in the air. "Bombs away!"

Jason threw a toy Arabian horse at Mike. "Attack!" he cried.

Mike laughed and flung an Appaloosa across the room. "It's a bird. . . . It's a plane. . . . It's Superhorse!"

"Stop!" Mari cried out.

Mrs. Reynolds leaped from her seat. "Mike and Jason, pick up those horses! The two of you are staying after school."

Mike and Jason each picked up a horse from the floor. Brenda and Alison found two others. They all put the horses back inside the duffel bag on Julia's desk.

"Now apologize," Mrs. Reynolds said, frowning at the boys.

"Sorry, Mari," the boys muttered.

"That was a fine presentation, Mari," Mrs. Reynolds said as Mari lugged her bag back to her seat. "All right, everyone. It's time for us to pack up and go home."

As the class gathered their things, Nancy walked over to Mari. "Great show-and-tell," she said. "Your horses are really cool."

But Mari wasn't listening. She was searching through her duffel bag.

"What's wrong, Mari?" Nancy asked.

"It's Silvermane!" Mari cried out. "She's gone!"

2

The Search for Silvermane

"Somebody stole Silvermane!" Mari burst into tears.

Mrs. Reynolds made her way over to Mari. "Did you search your bag carefully?" The teacher looked through the duffel bag.

"It isn't here," she said finally. "No one is leaving until this classroom is searched from top to bottom."

The class groaned.

"Come on," Mrs. Reynolds said, clapping her hands. "Start looking. I want that unicorn found."

The class spread out to look.

"Who cares if her dumb old unicorn is missing?" Nancy heard Brenda say. "She's a show-off anyway."

Alison looked under a chair. "Can't we look tomorrow?" she asked. "It's past three o'clock."

George turned to her. "If you want to go home, then find Silvermane."

"We will," Brenda said, moving closer to Alison. "And when we do, I'll write all about it in the *Carlton News.*"

Brenda's father helped her make a newspaper on their home computer. Nancy thought the *Carlton News* was just like Brenda—mean and gossipy.

Nancy started looking through a cluttered bookshelf. Maybe the boys threw the unicorn over here, she thought. Then she remembered that Mari didn't pass Silvermane around. The boys couldn't have thrown it.

Maybe Mari was right, Nancy thought. Maybe someone *did* steal it.

Julia was close by, looking near Mrs.

Reynolds's desk. "What do you think Mrs. Reynolds will do to the person who took the unicorn?" she asked Nancy.

"They'll probably get in big trouble." Nancy started looking by the teacher's desk, too. Then she noticed something on the floor. "Wait a minute, Julia," Nancy said. "What's that under your shoe?"

Julia lifted her foot. Nancy picked up a small plastic comb with a silver *S* painted on it.

"It's Silvermane's," Julia said, staring at the comb. "How did that get there?"

Maybe you were hiding it, Nancy thought. She gave the comb to Mrs. Reynolds.

The class searched for a little while longer. But the unicorn was nowhere to be found.

Mrs. Reynolds sighed. "All right, everyone. Get your things together and line up to go home. I'm sorry, Mari. I'm sure we'll find your unicorn tomorrow. In the meantime, I'll alert the Lost and Found, okay?"

"Okay." Mari sniffled. Her eyes were red and puffy from crying.

Mrs. Reynolds looked around the room. It was crowded with all kinds of science, art, and show-and-tell projects. "What a mess," she said. "No wonder Silvermane is lost. I'm going to have to stay after school to do some cleaning."

Nancy almost jumped out of her chair. "I'll help!" Then she leaned over to Bess, who sat at the desk next to her. "I want to stay and look for clues," Nancy whispered. "That unicorn couldn't have just disappeared."

Brenda heard her. "Oh, brother," she said. "Nancy thinks she's a detective again."

"She *is* a detective!" George shouted from her seat. "You're just jealous."

"I bet I can find out what really happened to that unicorn before Nancy does," Brenda said.

"You're always saying things like that," George said. "And you never do."

Brenda's face turned red. She looked ready to explode.

"Girls! Stop arguing this instant," Mrs. Reynolds commanded. "Nancy, if you'd really like to help me clean up, you may. But first call home from the telephone in the main office to get permission."

"Can we stay, too?" George and Bess asked.

"Yes, if you call home and get permission," Mrs. Reynolds said. "Now, let's walk out to the yard for dismissal. I want Nancy, Bess, George, Mike, and Jason to stay by me. We'll all be coming back to the room together."

As the class walked down the stairs, Nancy felt someone from behind tap her arm. She turned to see Mari's hopeful face. "Are you really a detective?" Mari asked.

"Yes," Nancy said. "I've solved lots of cases."

"Will you help me find my unicorn?" Mari said.

Bess placed a hand on the new girl's shoulder. "Don't worry, Mari. You'll have your unicorn back in no time."

Nancy hoped in her heart that Bess was right.

After dismissal, Nancy, Bess, and George called their homes. They were all allowed to stay after school. Later the Drews' housekeeper, Hannah Gruen, would pick up the three girls and drive them home.

"Meet me at the Double Dip," Hannah told Nancy over the phone. "You can all have a little ice cream while you wait for me."

"Thanks, Hannah!" Nancy said. She hung up the receiver.

Mrs. Reynolds phoned Mike's and Jason's homes. Then she led the way back to the classroom. "Just a minute," she told the girls. "Let me deal with these two first."

She faced Mike and Jason and told them they would have to write about what they did wrong. "Use up both sides of your paper," she said.

The boys went to their desks.

"All right, volunteers." Mrs. Reynolds smiled at the girls. "It's time to clean."

Bess sighed.

Nancy knew why. Bess hated to get dirty.

"I'm only doing this to help Mari," Bess said to Nancy. Then Bess looked at Mrs. Reynolds. "And help you, too, of course," she added with a smile.

Mrs. Reynolds patted Bess on the shoulder. "I think you'll be able to search for Silvermane and help me clean at the same time," she said.

"Where would you like us to start?" Nancy asked.

"Take those stacks of construction paper from the windowsill and put them neatly in the supply closet, please," Mrs. Reynolds said.

No one had looked in the closet, Nancy thought. Maybe someone hid Silvermane in there.

Nancy grabbed the paper and walked inside the big closet. She put the paper on an empty shelf. Then she checked the other shelves. She saw boxes of chalk, rolled-up charts, and some textbooks wrapped in plastic.

Nancy's shoulders slumped. "There's no unicorn in here."

As Nancy turned to leave the closet, she saw Mike looking inside Mari's desk. Mrs. Reynolds was busy going through some papers. She didn't see him.

He looks like he just did something sneaky, Nancy thought as she watched Mike straighten up and glance around the classroom. Then he tiptoed back to his desk and gave Jason a thumbs-up signal.

What are those boys up to? Nancy wondered, stepping out of the closet.

She checked to see what her two friends were doing. Bess was erasing the chalkboard, and George was lining up the desks into neater rows.

I bet no one else saw him, Nancy thought. *I'd better find out what he did.*

"Nancy," Mrs. Reynolds called before Nancy had a chance to look inside Mari's desk.

Nancy walked over to the teacher.

Mrs. Reynolds handed Nancy a pile of used paper. "Could you toss these in the recycling bin?"

When Nancy threw the stack into the blue plastic pail, she caught sight of a large ball of paper. *What's this?* she thought as she reached inside the bin and pulled it out.

Nancy unraveled the top sheet. It was an old copy of the *Carlton News.* Then she unwrapped the rest and gasped.

Nestled inside the crumpled paper was a plastic stand that had one word printed across it: Silvermane.

3

A Very Nice Suspect

Nancy gave Silvermane's stand to Mrs. Reynolds.

"It looks as though the unicorn really was stolen," Mrs. Reynolds said, shaking her head. She put the stand in one of the drawers of her desk.

Then Mrs. Reynolds looked around the classroom. "Our room looks great. Thanks for your help, girls," she said. "Especially you, Nancy. Good work finding Silvermane's stand."

Nancy, Bess, and George grabbed their knapsacks and said goodbye to Mrs. Reynolds. Mike and Jason were still working on their essays when the girls headed out to the Double Dip.

"Poor Mari," Bess said as the three girls left the school. "I can't believe someone in our class stole Silvermane."

"Yeah," George said. "What a crummy way to start her first week at a new school. She must hate it here."

"We've got to get that unicorn back," Nancy said.

At the Double Dip the girls ordered an ice cream sundae to share. George carried the sundae, Bess carried three spoons, and Nancy led the way to a little table by the window.

As they sat down, Nancy took out her detective's notebook and her favorite purple pen from her knapsack.

Nancy's father had given her the special notebook to use just for solving mysteries. It had a shiny blue cover.

She turned to a clean page. On the top she wrote, "The Missing Unicorn Mystery."

"Let's think of who would want to

take the unicorn and why," Nancy said. "I already have a few ideas."

Farther down the page, Nancy wrote the word "Suspects." On the top of the list Nancy wrote two names—Mike Minelli and Jason Hutchings.

Bess frowned when she saw their names. "I bet they did it."

George scooped up some ice cream. "Maybe the boys took the unicorn as a joke. They're always up to something."

"They even told Mari to watch out." Nancy rested her chin in her hand. "And when I looked for Silvermane in the supply closet, I saw Mike snooping around Mari's desk."

"I told you they did it," Bess said.

Nancy tasted a spoonful of the sundae. "I bet they took the unicorn when they put the horses back in Mari's bag."

"But Brenda and Alison put horses back in Mari's bag, too," George said.

"That's true," Nancy said. "We'd better put them on the list." Nancy wrote down their names.

"I don't know about Alison, but Brenda is mean enough to have taken the unicorn," George said.

"Especially since Brenda doesn't like Mari," Nancy said. "She thinks Mari's stuck-up, remember?"

"She does?" Bess plucked the cherry off the top of the sundae. "That settles it. Brenda must have done it."

"Don't forget what was wrapped around Silvermane's stand," Nancy said.

"The *Carlton News!*" George and Bess cried together.

"That doesn't prove Brenda did it," Nancy said. "It could just have been someone's copy of the paper. But it's still a clue."

"What about Alison?" George asked. "She's been nice to Mari."

"Alison is Brenda's best friend. If Brenda took the unicorn, Alison probably knows about it. But she might not want to tattle. Let's keep her on the list for now."

Nancy put a question mark next to Alison's name. "A real detective doesn't take someone off the list just because they're nice." Nancy looked at her friends. "My last suspect is *very* nice."

"Who is it?" Bess asked.

"Julia Santos," Nancy said. She wrote the name in her book.

"No way." George dropped her spoon on the table. "Julia's great. She's on our soccer team, Nancy. She'd never do a mean thing like steal something."

"Didn't you hear Julia say how much she wanted a Silvermane unicorn?" Nancy said. "Maybe she wanted it enough to take it."

Bess gasped. "You're right! Julia must have done it!"

Nancy couldn't help smiling. "You think they *all* did it, Bess."

"I mean it, this time," Bess said. "Remember? Mari wouldn't even let Julia touch Silvermane. Maybe Mari hurt Julia's feelings."

"Julia was near the bag—and the unicorn—the whole time," Nancy added. "And there's one other thing. I found Silvermane's comb under Julia's foot. I think she was trying to hide it."

After writing down her suspects, Nancy began another list. She titled it "Clues." Underneath she wrote:

1. The comb. Found near Julia.
2. The stand. Someone threw it out on purpose.
3. The *Carlton News*. Whoever threw out the stand probably reads Brenda's paper.

Nancy sighed. "*Everybody* reads Brenda's paper."

Just then a voice called out, "Hi, girls."

Nancy looked up to see Hannah by the door.

"Come on," Hannah said, waving the car keys. "Let's head on home."

During the car ride, Nancy told Hannah about the missing unicorn mystery.

"It sounds as if you're on the job again," Hannah said, keeping her eyes on the road. "Just remember to be careful."

"I will," Nancy said. "And I promise to keep a cool head the way Daddy always tells me to."

The next day Nancy almost forgot her promise. On the way to school, she saw Brenda running toward her.

Brenda had a big smile on her face. When she reached Nancy she had to catch her breath before she announced, "I did it! I solved the mystery before you!"

Brenda waved a copy of the *Carlton News* in front of Nancy's face. "I wrote all about it. Read it and weep." She shoved the newspaper into Nancy's hand.

CARLTON NEWS
MISSING UNICORN
MYSTERY
SOLVED!
CARLTON NEWS

Nancy stopped in the middle of the sidewalk and read:

MISSING UNICORN MYSTERY
SOLVED!
by Brenda Carlton

Who would believe that the daughter of our school's very own soccer coach would steal anything? But it's true, and I saw the proof with my own eyes! Julia Santos is a thief!

4

The Camera Doesn't Lie

"What do you mean Julia is a thief?" Nancy stopped reading and frowned at Brenda. "What proof do you have?"

"It's right in your hand," Brenda said. "Look at the picture in my article."

Nancy glanced back down at the newspaper. There was a picture of Silvermane, all right, standing right on top of someone's kitchen counter. On the wall behind the unicorn was a clock shaped like a sunflower. Nancy's heart sank. She had seen that clock before—at Julia's house.

"I took that picture through Julia's back window," Brenda said. "Just like a real reporter."

"What were you doing sneaking around Julia's house?" Nancy asked.

"I was looking for clues," Brenda said. "I didn't think I would find the unicorn so fast. But I knew Julia was guilty all along."

Nancy gripped the newspaper tightly, crumpling it a bit. "And just how did you figure that out?" she asked.

"Come on, Nancy," Brenda said. "Everyone knew Julia was dying to have a unicorn just like Mari's. Everyone saw how snobby Mari was to her about touching it."

Nancy didn't know what to say next.

"I told you I was going to solve this mystery first." Brenda patted the stack of sheets she had tucked into her book bag. "Now I have a newspaper to give out."

Brenda turned to go, then stopped and looked over her shoulder at Nancy.

"I can't wait to see Julia's face," she said. "If she looks even half as shocked as you do, Nancy, it'll be *really* funny." Brenda laughed and ran toward school.

Nancy stood on the sidewalk, watching Brenda. I can't believe she solved the mystery, Nancy thought, gritting her teeth. Brenda doesn't keep track of the suspects or clues or anything! She doesn't even have a special notebook!

Nancy stuffed the article in her pocket. Julia was sure to be in big trouble, Nancy thought. Brenda's newspaper would be all over school in no time.

By the time class began, many of the kids in Mrs. Reynolds's class had read Brenda's article. They were whispering to each other about it.

Mrs. Reynolds had to tell the class to settle down before she spoke.

"Yesterday Mari lost her unicorn. At the end of the day, Nancy found Silvermane's stand and comb. I hope that by the end of the week the unicorn itself will be found and returned to Mari. That's all I'm going to say about it for now," she said. "Let's begin class."

By lunchtime everyone in the cafeteria was talking about Brenda's article.

"I can't believe it," George said as she waited with Nancy in the lunch line. "I didn't think Julia would ever steal."

Bess was standing behind George. "Now that everyone knows she took the unicorn, Julia has to bring it back."

Nancy watched Julia join the back of the line. "I'm going to go talk to her," she told Bess and George. She left her friends and walked over to Julia.

"Are you in the mood for mystery meat, Julia?" Nancy chuckled. "That's what they're serving today."

The students always called the thin slices of meat drowned in brown gravy "mystery meat." Even after tasting it, no one knew what kind of meat it was supposed to be.

Julia looked up at Nancy. Nancy could tell Julia had been crying.

"I didn't take Mari's unicorn," Julia said. "You've got to believe me."

"But what about Brenda's proof?" Nancy asked.

"The unicorn in that picture is mine," Julia insisted.

"But yesterday you said you didn't have one," Nancy said.

"My mom surprised me with a Silvermane unicorn after school yesterday, because I've been getting good grades. I keep trying to explain this to the other kids, but no one will listen."

Nancy looked closely at Julia's tear-stained face. "I believe you. And I'm going to find out who really took Silvermane."

The two girls were served their lunches. When they saw the mystery-meat sandwiches, they wrinkled their noses and laughed. Looking for seats, they walked past Brenda's table.

Brenda was talking to a group of kids

MILK

sitting at her lunch table. "I was smart enough to bring my camera along," she said, "so I took a picture. I practically caught Julia red-handed."

Julia stopped walking and stared at Brenda. "That's it," she mumbled under her breath, and marched over to Brenda.

Before Nancy could stop her, Julia had turned her lunch tray upside-down—and dumped her mystery-meat sandwich all over Brenda's head!

5

Mystery Meat Mess

Brenda sat frozen in place as gravy dripped down her face and hair.

The entire room burst out laughing.

Nancy covered her mouth to hide her smile. She noticed Mike and Jason at the next table. They were holding their stomachs from laughing so hard.

"Meat-head! Meat-head!" Jason chanted at Brenda as he pounded his fist on his lunch table.

Even the students who had been listening to Brenda's story just a minute before were now howling.

"Meat-head! Meat-head!" they all joined in.

Alison was sitting next to Brenda. She tried to help Brenda clean up the mystery meat mess. By then the whole cafeteria was chanting, "Meat-head! Meat-head! Meat-head!"

Nancy thought Brenda looked as if she was about to cry. Nancy almost felt sorry for her.

Just then Ms. Rodriguez, a teacher on cafeteria duty, stepped forward. "Let's go," she said, taking both Julia and Brenda by the arm. "The assistant principal will want to see you." She looked at Nancy. "You, too."

Nancy had never had to go to Mrs. Oshida's office before. Even though she hadn't done anything wrong, Nancy was nervous.

She swallowed hard and followed Ms. Rodriguez down the long hall. The closer she got to the door of the office, the more Nancy wished the hallway was longer.

Ms. Rodriguez knocked on Mrs. Oshida's door and led the girls inside.

“What have we here?” Mrs. Oshida asked, looking at Brenda. “A food fight?”

“She dumped her lunch all over my head—” Brenda began.

“She lied about me to the whole school—” Julia said at the same time.

“Wait a minute,” Mrs. Oshida said, holding up her hand. “One at a time.”

Ms. Rodriguez pointed to Nancy. “This girl saw the whole thing.”

Mrs. Oshida looked over the top of her reading glasses at Nancy. “Nancy Drew, you’re a very good student. You tell me what happened.”

Nancy took a deep breath and explained all about how Mari’s unicorn had disappeared. Then she told Mrs. Oshida about Brenda’s article and how angry it had made Julia.

“Because,” Nancy said, “Julia didn’t take Silvermane.”

“How can you say that?” Brenda pointed to a copy of the newspaper she had brought along. “I proved it!”

"Let me see that," Mrs. Oshida said.

Brenda gave her the paper.

Nancy took her copy of the *Carlton News* out of her pocket and looked at it.

"I just figured out the *real* proof in this article," Nancy said. "And it shows that Julia didn't steal Silvermane."

"What are you talking about?" Brenda asked.

"The unicorn in this picture is *standing* on the counter. Mari's missing unicorn wouldn't be able to do that. I found her Silvermane stand yesterday in our classroom. Mrs. Reynolds has it."

Brenda covered her face with her hands.

"And you can call my mom," Julia said. "She'll tell you that unicorn is mine."

Julia's mother was the school soccer coach. Her office was next to the gym.

Mrs. Oshida quickly called Coach Santos. When she hung up the phone,

CARLTON NEWS
MISSING
MYSTERY
SOLVED!

the assistant principal sighed and looked at Brenda.

"Brenda, your father is a well-known newspaperman in this town," she said. "He knows how important it is for newspaper articles to be just about the facts. Your article wasn't all facts, was it?"

"But I *thought* it was," Brenda said.

"And as for you, young lady," Mrs. Oshida said, turning to Julia, "your mother works for this school. She's very disappointed in your actions today."

Julia hung her head.

Mrs. Oshida tapped her fingers on her desktop for a moment. "This is what I'm going to do," she said. "As punishment, neither one of you will enjoy recess this afternoon. Instead, you will spend that time in the art room making apology cards for each other. Is that understood?"

Brenda and Julia nodded.

That sounds fair, Nancy thought.

"That's not all," the assistant principal said. "In your next newspaper, Brenda, you are to write another story about the missing unicorn. This time, you will write about how you were wrong."

Brenda squirmed.

"And you, Julia, will pay for Brenda's lunch tomorrow," Mrs. Oshida added.

"Okay," Julia said.

Mrs. Oshida looked at the three girls for a moment. "You are all dismissed."

Ms. Rodriguez led Brenda and Julia to the art room.

Nancy was allowed to go to recess. She ran out to the schoolyard and found George, Bess, and Mari playing jump rope. They stopped when they saw her.

"What happened, Nancy?" Bess asked.

Nancy told them everything that had happened in the assistant principal's office.

"I really thought Julia took Silvermane," Mari said.

"We all did," George said. "Just because of Brenda's dumb article."

"But it was nice of Brenda to want to help find Silvermane," Mari said.

"That's just it," Nancy said. "Brenda doesn't usually do nice things. Maybe she wrote that article so that we would all think Julia did it—"

"But instead it was really Brenda?" George cut in. "That would be sneaky."

"That sounds like Brenda," Bess said.

"So I guess that means she's still a suspect," George said.

"At least I can take Julia off my list," Nancy said. "Unless . . ."

"Unless what?" Mari asked.

"Unless Julia stole the unicorn before she knew her mother had bought her one."

"Wow," Bess said. "I would *never* have thought of that."

Nancy groaned and flopped to the ground. "This is awful," she said. "I'm right back where I started. I still have the same suspects. And no new clues."

"What about this?" Mari handed Nancy a piece of paper.

On it was a drawing of a unicorn. A speech balloon coming from its mouth read: "Help! I've been horse-napped!"

"Where did you get this?" Nancy asked.

"I found it in my desk this morning," Mari said.

Nancy snapped her fingers. "This is from Mike and Jason. I knew they put something in your desk yesterday."

"Those two creeps," Bess muttered.

At the same time, the bell for the end of recess rang. Nancy, Bess, George, and Mari lined up with the rest of their class.

Nancy dropped her voice to a whisper as Mrs. Reynolds led them all back to the classroom. "I'll talk to Mike and Jason after school. Don't worry, Mari. We'll get to the bottom of this."

After all the students had settled into

their seats, Mrs. Reynolds sat down at her desk.

"I heard about what happened in the cafeteria today," she said. "This unicorn problem has gone far enough. From now on this class will never have show-and-tell again."

6

Superballs and Flower Fairies

"That's not fair!" Mike stood up. "Almost everyone has shown their stuff. Now I'll miss my turn!"

"Can't we just finish this week's show-and-tell, Mrs. Reynolds?" Bess folded her hands together. "Pleeeeease?"

"Yeah," Mike said. "Can we?"

"Pleeeeease," the whole class repeated.

"All right, class," Mrs. Reynolds said. "We'll finish up this time. But then that's it for show-and-tell."

Nancy realized that the whole class loved show-and-tell as much as she did. Maybe Mrs. Reynolds will change her mind if the unicorn is found, Nancy thought. I've got to solve this case.

That afternoon it was Mike Minelli's turn for show-and-tell. He walked up to a table set up in the front of the room.

Mike held up a small, rainbow-colored rubber ball. "This is a one-of-a-kind super bouncing ball," he said. "I made it with the help of the Ricochet Ball Kit."

Mike pointed to the boxes and a big bowl of water set up on a table. "I have three kits right here, and I need a few volunteers."

With Mrs. Reynolds's permission, Mike picked Jason, George, and Peter DeSands.

"Okay," Mike said. "Pour some of the colored sand from these bottles into your ball mold. You can use as many colors as you want."

Nancy watched as George filled her mold with purple and yellow sand.

Then she shook the mold so the colors swirled together.

"Now snap your molds closed and put them in this bowl of warm water for a few minutes," Mike said.

Jason, George, and Peter placed their molds inside the bowl. When the superballs were ready, the volunteers opened their molds. Out popped three perfect balls.

"Ta-da!" Mike sang. He gathered the balls from his volunteers. "Now watch this." Mike bounced the balls against the chalkboard. Before the class knew what was happening, rainbow-colored balls were zooming all over the room!

They bounced against the ceiling, zipped over heads, and knocked over projects. Some students screamed. Some kids laughed. Others covered their heads or ducked under desks.

Mrs. Reynolds jumped up from where she had been sitting in the back of the room, and rushed to the front. "Calm

down, class. Mike, collect those balls and give them to me."

"But—" Mike began.

"No buts, Mike," Mrs. Reynolds said. "We'll talk about your getting them back after school."

Mike did what he was told.

Soon the class had quieted down. In a tired voice, Mrs. Reynolds called on the next student. "Alison Wegman."

Nancy sat at attention. Alison had promised to show something really special. Nancy couldn't wait to see what it was. When Alison took out her Flower Fairy perfume, Nancy was disappointed.

"Not that," Mike complained. "We've all seen it."

"And *smelled* it," Jason added.

Alison held her chin up. "I *was* going to bring in something else," she said. "But *somebody* stole my idea."

What's that supposed to mean? Nancy wondered.

Alison cleared her throat. "This is my Flower Fairy perfume. As you can see, the crystal bottle is in the shape of a fairy. The commercials say, 'With one spray, you will smell like a spring bouquet.' It's special because my mother bought it for me and no one else I know has it." Alison seemed to have run out of things to say. "Can I pass it around?" she asked Mrs. Reynolds.

"You may," Mrs. Reynolds said.

Alison handed the perfume to Julia Santos. Julia looked at the bottle and then passed the perfume to Brenda. Brenda smiled at her.

While Brenda was looking at the bottle, Mike leaned over from his seat.

"Psst! Hurry up, *Meathead,*" he said.

Brenda tightened her lips. She pointed the bottle at Mike and sprayed him!

"Oops," she said with a smile. "Sorry. It was an accident."

Mike jumped to his feet. A look of horror was on his face. "Arrrgh, I smell like flowers!"

"You mean a 'spring bouquet.' "

Brenda giggled and the whole class laughed.

Mike began to sneeze. That made the class laugh even harder.

Mrs. Reynolds strode to the front of the room and took the perfume from Brenda's hand. "That's enough." She gave the bottle back to Alison. "Please sit down," she told her. "I need to speak with the class."

Alison quickly took her seat.

Mrs. Reynolds leaned against her desk and faced the students. She studied their faces for a few moments. Then she spoke.

"Boys and girls," she said, "I meant what I said earlier. But I don't want to punish the entire class for something one student did."

Or maybe two kids, Nancy thought, looking over at Mike and Jason.

Mrs. Reynolds continued. "I hope the person who *borrowed* Mari's unicorn—for whatever reason—is finished using it. That person has two more days to return it: tomorrow and Friday."

Mrs. Reynolds pointed to her desk. "The unicorn may be left right here. I don't need to know who did it. It just needs to be returned to Mari safe and sound. No questions will be asked."

Mrs. Reynolds smiled. "I have always thought of you as a great class that got along well. I hope I'm right. Class dismissed."

The class was silent as they packed up to leave.

Nancy watched Jason and Mike go to their cubbies and collect their things. This is my chance to question them, she thought.

Nancy dashed out of the classroom and walked up behind them. She was about to talk to them but stopped when she heard what they were saying.

"So when do you think we should do it?" Jason asked Mike. "Tomorrow or Friday?"

"Tomorrow," Mike replied. "The sooner the better. How about at recess?"

"Mari will sure be surprised," Mike said.

Nancy stayed where she was and let the boys walk away. She didn't want them to know she had heard everything.

Nancy went to her cubby. *The boys are bringing the unicorn back tomorrow,* she thought as she grabbed her things. *And I know just how to catch them in the act!*

7

Real Detectives

"Did you just say you want to have a stakeout?" George asked Nancy.

"That's right," Nancy said.

"What do we have to do?" Bess asked.

"We have to wait for the bad guys. Just like real detectives," Nancy said.

Bess and George were staying at Nancy's house for dinner. They were in her room, sitting on her bed. Nancy had just told them what she'd heard Mike and Jason say earlier at school.

Nancy's eyes sparkled with excitement. "We can sneak into the classroom and hide before the boys get there. That way we can catch them when they bring back the unicorn."

"Catch them?" Bess asked. She hugged one of Nancy's pillows. "You mean grab them or something?"

"No," Nancy said. "I mean see them with our own eyes. That way we'll really know they took the unicorn. My father says a good detective must always be sure."

"Then what?" George asked. "Mrs. Reynolds said she didn't care who took Silvermane—she just wanted it back."

"We'll tell Mari," Nancy said. "She has the right to know who did it, don't you think?"

"I guess if it was my unicorn, I'd want to know who stole it," Bess said.

Nancy opened her notebook to the page where she had written down her suspects and clues for the missing unicorn mystery. On a new line she wrote, "The Plan."

Then she thought for a moment. "I think we should hide in the supply closet," she said. "It's pretty big, and we can all fit if we squeeze in together. We can leave the door open a little and peek out. That way we can see what happens, but no one will see us."

George pointed to Nancy's notebook. "Write that down, Nancy," George said. "But how do we get into the classroom in the first place? No one is allowed up there at lunchtime."

"We'll have to run back up when no one's looking," Nancy said.

She wrote, "Sneak into classroom."

"What about lunch?" Bess asked. "I don't want to miss that, even for a stakeout. Maybe we should bring lunch from home and eat it very fast before going upstairs."

"Good idea, Bess," Nancy said. She quickly wrote down, "Lunch from home."

"Dinner is served!" Hannah called out, knocking on the door.

"It smells delicious, Hannah," Nancy said. "We'll be right down." Nancy turned back to her friends. "Then it's settled. Tomorrow we'll have our stakeout."

The next afternoon at lunchtime, Nancy, Bess, and George were all crammed into the supply closet of their classroom.

"There just isn't . . . enough . . . room in here," Bess said between grunts.

"Stop complaining," George whispered. "It's easier if you stay still."

"Shhh!" Nancy hissed. "Don't talk. You could ruin everything."

It was dark and dusty in Mrs. Reynolds's supply closet.

"Uh-oh," Bess said.

"What is it?" George asked.

"I have a tickle in my throat," Bess said.

"Don't cough now!" George cried.

"Shhh!" Nancy said again. She was bent over and had opened the closet door just a crack. She had a clear view

GLUE

of Mrs. Reynolds's desk. She'd be able to see everything.

Bess and George were quiet for a few minutes. Then Bess shouted, "Ow!"

Nancy spun around. "What's the matter?"

"George stepped on my foot!" Bess said.

George frowned. "It was an accident!"

Nancy quickly peeked at Mrs. Reynolds's desk again. The top was still clear. "Phew, I didn't miss it," she said. Then she looked back at Bess and George. "Now, *don't move.*"

The girls were very still for a long time.

"Nancy," Bess whispered.

"What?" Nancy asked.

"I still have a tickle in my throat," Bess said.

Nancy turned to look at Bess. "Well, can you cough quietly?"

"I'll try." Bess cleared her throat. "Maybe if I get behind George it won't sound so loud." She pushed George aside. "Excuse me."

"Ouch! Now you're on *my* foot!" George pushed Bess back.

"Whoa!" Bess cried. She lost her balance and bumped into Nancy.

With a yelp, Nancy fell against the door of the closet and tumbled out—straight into Brenda Carlton!

8

The Return of Silvermane

Brenda!" Nancy shrieked.

"Nancy!" Brenda shouted back as they crashed to the floor.

They sat there, staring at each other, their legs tangled together.

"Don't just sit there," Brenda said. "Get off me!"

Nancy untangled herself from Brenda.

"What were you doing in there?" Brenda demanded, dusting off her jeans.

"What were you doing out *here?*" Nancy asked Brenda.

"I was looking for you," Brenda said.

"I knew you were up to something, so I followed you. What's your story?"

Before Nancy could reply, Bess tugged on Nancy's sleeve.

"Nancy—look!" She pointed to Mrs. Reynolds's desk.

The unicorn was lying on top of it.

Nancy's mouth dropped open.

George turned to Brenda. "You *did* take Silvermane! And you blamed Julia! Of all the dirty, rotten—"

"I didn't!" Brenda insisted. "I don't know how that unicorn got there!"

George squinted. "Sure."

Nancy led the way to Mrs. Reynolds's desk. As the girls gathered around her, she picked up the unicorn and touched its tail. Then she turned it over, looking very closely for clues. "I think Brenda's telling the truth," she said.

"She can't be," Bess said. "Who else could have done it?"

Nancy took a deep breath and said, "Alison."

"You're crazy," Brenda said. "My best friend is not a thief."

Nancy headed out of the classroom. "Let's go ask her."

The girls found Alison in the schoolyard, playing hopscotch with Mari.

Mari looked up first. "I was just wondering where all of you w—" She caught sight of the unicorn in Nancy's hands and gasped. "Is that *my* Silvermane?" she asked.

"Yes." Nancy handed it to her.

Mari kissed the unicorn on the nose. "Where did you find it?"

Nancy faced Alison. "Why don't you *you* tell her what happened, Alison?" she asked.

"What do you mean?" Alison asked.

Brenda stepped next to her friend. "Nancy thinks you're the one who took it," she said. "Can you believe that?"

Alison laughed. "That's funny."

"I don't think it's funny that Silvermane smells just like Flower Fairy perfume," Nancy said.

"What?" Brenda asked.

Alison stopped laughing.

Mari sniffed her toy. "Nancy's right," she said.

"Let me smell that," Brenda demanded. She grabbed the unicorn and sniffed its tail. "It's true," she said in a small voice. She looked over at her best friend. "Alison?"

"Why would I have to steal Mari's unicorn," Alison said, "when I have a—" She stopped.

"Silvermane of your own?" Nancy finished for her.

"How did you know?" Alison asked.

"I figured out your hint," Nancy said. "You were planning to show *your* Silvermane for your show-and-tell surprise."

"That's right," George said to Alison. "You said your show-and-tell was going to be silver and white."

"But my surprise was ruined when Mari showed up with Silvermane first."

Alison turned to the new girl. "So I got mad. You copied me, Mari."

Mari didn't say anything.

"I was so angry, I took your Silvermane," Alison said. "I figured since you stole my idea, I would steal your unicorn. I'm sorry, Mari."

"But Mari didn't steal your idea," Bess said.

Mari looked down at the ground.

"I wanted to give her back to you," Alison insisted. "But Mrs. Reynolds was so upset, and Brenda and Julia got into that fight. And then I spilled my perfume all over Silvermane's tail. I didn't know what to do."

Mari slowly looked up at Alison. "I'm sorry, too," she said.

"What for?" Alison asked.

"Because I *did* steal your idea," Mari said. "I knew you were bringing in Silvermane for show-and-tell."

"How did you know?" Alison asked.

"Remember the first time we met—in the toy store?" Mari asked Alison.

"Yes," Alison said.

I heard you tell your mom about show-and-tell. I even saw you buy Silvermane," Mari said. "After you left, I asked my mom for Silvermane, too. I thought if I brought Silvermane to school that maybe the kids would like me."

"I liked you even before you brought in Silvermane," Nancy told Mari.

"So did I," Alison and Bess said together.

George looked sideways at Brenda. "Most of us did," George said. "You don't have to show off to make friends, Mari."

"Do you still want to be my friend?" Mari asked Alison.

Alison stuck out her hand. "If you still want to be mine."

The two girls shook hands.

"Hello, girls," a voice broke in.

The girls turned to see Mike and Jason.

Wait a minute, Nancy thought. If

they didn't take Silvermane, then what were they talking about yesterday?

Mike held out his hand to Brenda, and Jason held out his hand to Mari.

"I just want to say I'm sorry for calling you Meathead," Mike said.

"And I want to welcome you to our school," Jason told Mari.

"Okay," Mari said.

Brenda and Mari shook the boys' hands. Then they screamed. Mike and Jason's hands had broken off!

"They're fake!" Jason said between laughs.

"We had something *up our sleeves*. Get it?" Mike said. He was laughing so hard, tears came to his eyes.

"Very funny!" Brenda said. She picked up one of the fake hands and chased after Mike. "I'll get you!"

The girls all laughed.

When Nancy got home from school that day, she opened her notebook to The Missing Unicorn Mystery and wrote:

Today I learned that stealing an idea is just as bad as stealing a toy. Either way you can really hurt somebody's feelings.

Mari and Alison are giving each other a second chance to become friends. Mari told Mrs. Reynolds that she got her unicorn back. And Mrs. Reynolds said we could have show-and-tell again. She didn't even ask how Silvermane was returned. She was just glad that Mari was happy. And I'm glad the mystery was solved.

Case closed.

TAKE A RIDE WITH THE KIDS ON BUS FIVE!

Natalie Adams and James Penny have just started third grade. They like their teacher, and they like Maple Street School. The only trouble is, they have to ride bad old Bus Five to get there!

#1 THE BAD NEWS BULLY
Can Natalie and James stop the bully on Bus Five?

#2 WILD MAN AT THE WHEEL
When Mr. Balter calls in sick,
the kids get some strange new drivers.

#3 FINDERS KEEPERS
The kids on Bus Five keep losing things.
Is there a thief on board?

#4 I SURVIVED ON BUS FIVE
Bad luck turns into big fun
when Bus Five breaks down in a rainstorm.

BY MARCIA LEONARD
ILLUSTRATED BY JULIE DURRELL

Published by Pocket Books

1237-04